This
Disney
Classics Collection Storybook

b e l o n g s   t o

Aisling

DISNEY'S
ALICE
in
WONDERLAND
CLASSIC STORYBOOK

MOUSE WORKS

Published by Penguin Books Australia Ltd, 1998.
© 1998 Disney Enterprises, Inc.
Adapted by Catherine McCafferty
Illustrated by Atelier Philippe Harchy
Printed and bound in Hong Kong
0 7214 8732 7
5 7 9 10 8 6

CSRVAIW

The day was simply too splendid to spend listening to history lessons. While her sister read of kings and conquests, Alice wove a crown of daisies for her cat Dinah.

"Alice, will you kindly pay attention?" her sister said.

"I'm sorry," Alice answered. "But how can one possibly pay attention to a book with no pictures in it? In my world," she added, "books would be only pictures."

Alice slipped away from her sister. "Oh, Dinah!" she said. "In my world, all would be nonsense. Every animal would be just like a person. The flowers would talk to me, and the birds would be friends." Alice smiled. "It would be a wonderland."

As Alice dreamed of her wonderland, a rabbit scampered past. He was not just any rabbit. He was a white rabbit with a waistcoat and a watch—a rabbit who was just like a person!

"I'm late! I'm late! I'm late!" the White
Rabbit cried as he raced away.

Alice ran after him. "Mister Rabbit! Wait!"
she called.

"He must be going to something awfully
important, like a party or something," Alice
told Dinah. They hurried after the White
Rabbit until he disappeared down a rabbit hole.

Alice squeezed herself into the rabbit hole. As she crawled along, the tunnel became smaller and smaller. Alice struggled on. She wanted to find out why he was late, and what she was missing. The White Rabbit seemed to belong to the very world where she wanted to live.

Still, Alice knew that she should not be crawling down a rabbit tunnel. "After all," she explained to Dinah, "we haven't been invited. And curiosity can lead to—"

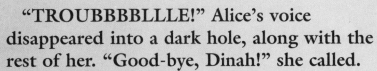

"TROUBBBBLLLE!" Alice's voice disappeared into a dark hole, along with the rest of her. "Good-bye, Dinah!" she called.

First Alice fell, then she floated, down, down, down through the darkness. "After this," she said to herself, "I shall think nothing of falling down stairs." She made out the shape of a lamp falling past her. Alice turned it on and looked around.

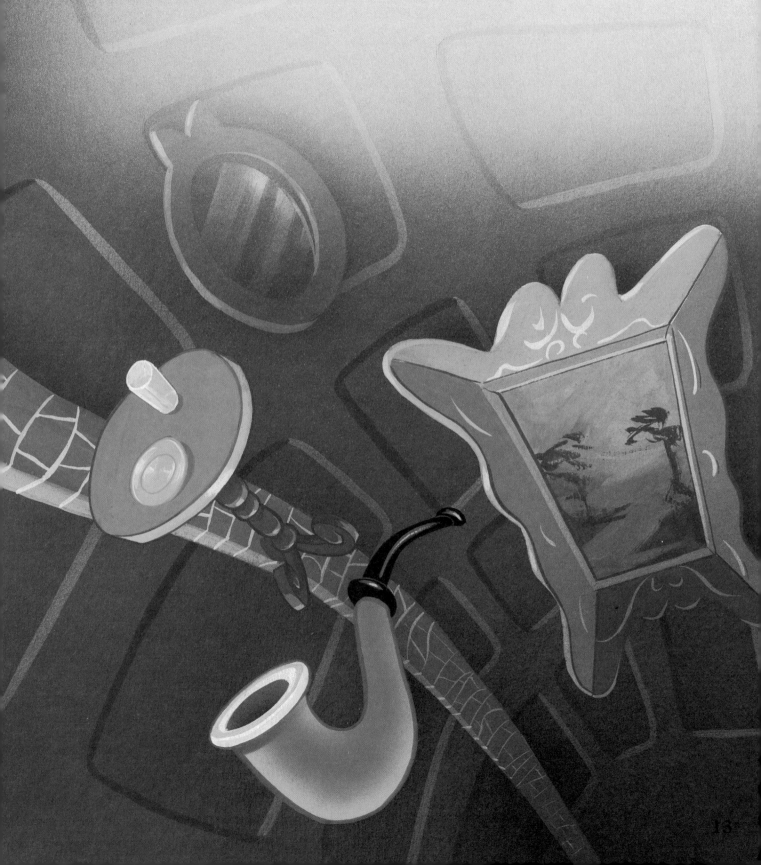

A book, a bottle, a picture, a pipe...pieces of everyday life floated past in a most peculiar manner. Even in her dreams of a nonsense world, Alice had not imagined a place like this. Why, an entire household hovered around her!

Then, with sudden speed, Alice landed upside down. A pair of right-side-up rabbit feet hurried past her.

Alice quickly turned herself right side up. "Wait, Mister Rabbit!" she called. As she raced behind him, the White Rabbit slipped through a door and slammed it behind him.

Alice kept following the rabbit. The next door was smaller. The door after that was smaller still. The doors became smaller and smaller, until finally, she couldn't fit through!

"Curiouser and curiouser," Alice said.

Alice twisted the knob on the last door. A nose wiggled under her fingers! "Oh, I beg your pardon!" she said.

"Quite all right," said the Doorknob, "but you did give me quite a turn." He laughed at his own joke.

What a strange place! Alice told the Doorknob about the White Rabbit, and asked if she could go through his door.

"Sorry," the Doorknob told her. "You're much too big."

"Try the bottle on the table," the Doorknob suggested.
Out of nowhere, a table with a bottle on it appeared.
"Drink Me" said the note on the bottle.

Alice went ahead and drank. What a yummy liquid—
cherry tart, custard, and pineapple! With each sip, Alice got
smaller and smaller. Now she would fit through the door!

"I forgot to say," the Doorknob chuckled. "I'm locked."

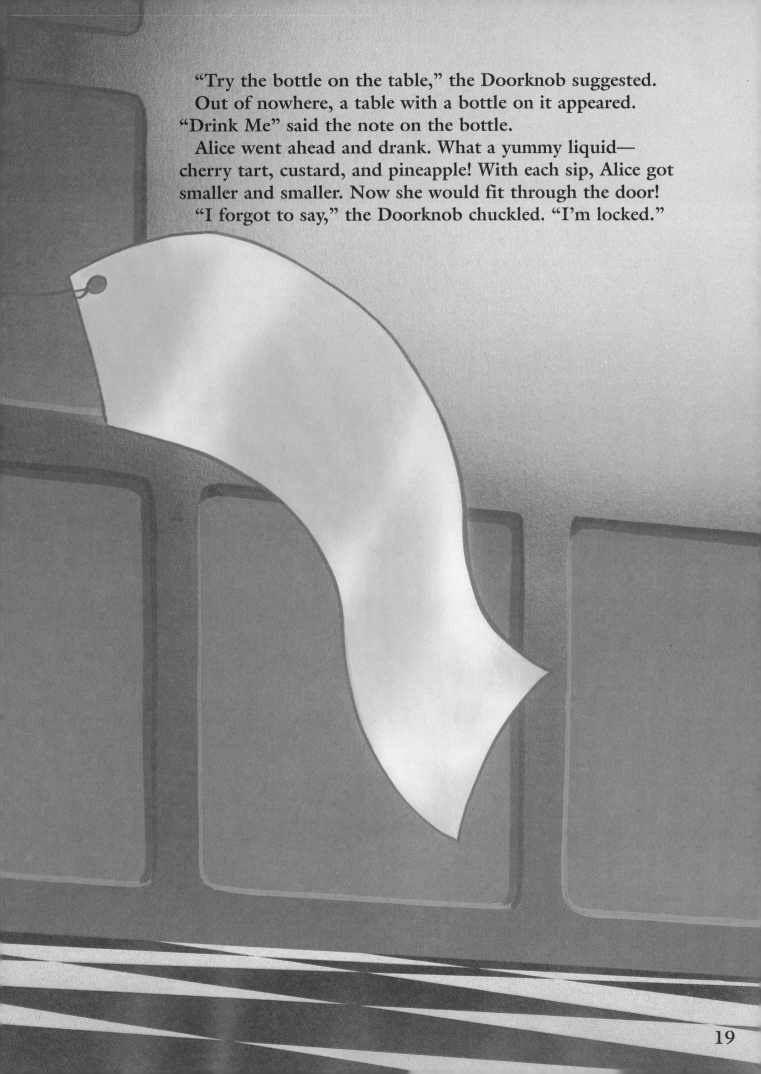

19

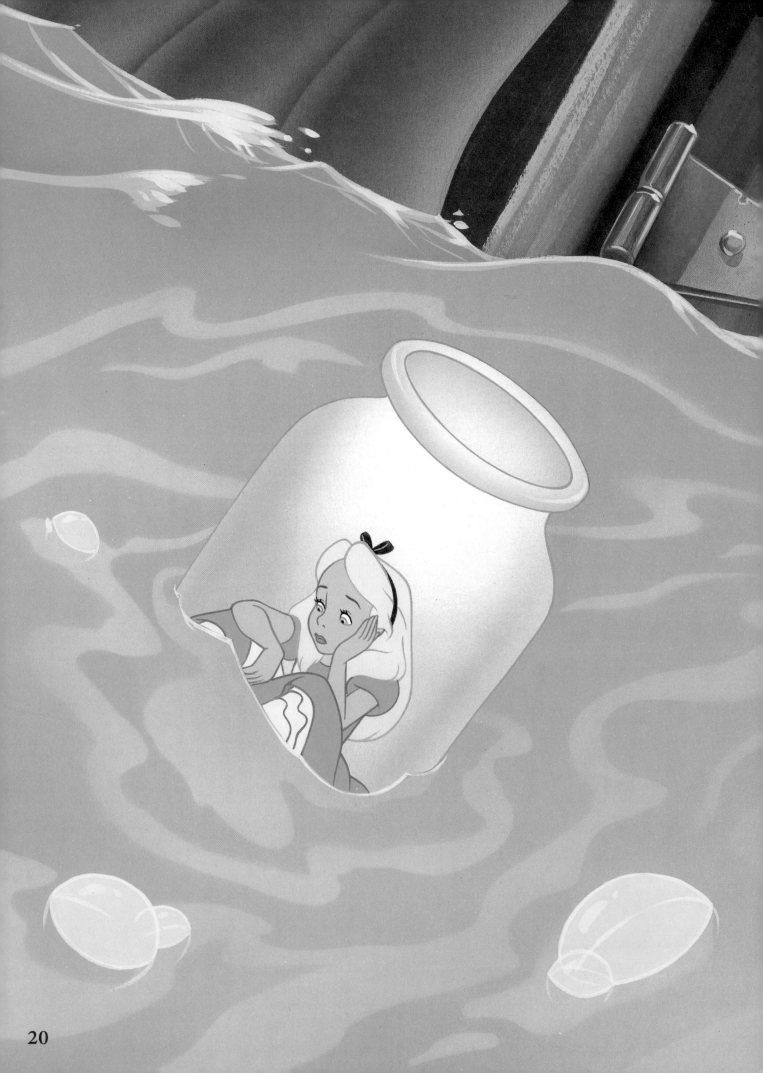

"Of course," he added, "there's a key."

High above tiny Alice, a key lay on the glass table. "Whatever will I do?" she said.

Suddenly a box appeared, and in it was a cookie labeled "Eat Me." Alice ate the cookie and grew into a giant. She would never fit through the door now! Her giant tears flooded the room.

Alarmed, the Doorknob told her to try the bottle again. Soon Alice was small enough to ride the bottle through the keyhole!

The waves swept Alice onto a beach, where a very odd race was taking place. Fish and birds ran round and round a dodo.

"You'll never get dry that way," the Dodo told her. "You have to join the race!"

Alice found herself in the race, but the waves washed over them again. "No one could get dry this way," Alice gasped.

Then she saw the White Rabbit. "Mister Rabbit!" she called as he ran off. "Oh, don't go away!"

Alice followed the White Rabbit deep into the woods. As she searched, two figures watched her silently. Turning, Alice found herself face to face with a peculiar pair of twins. "Tweedledee," she read on one collar. "Tweedledum," she read on the other.

Tweedledee and Tweedledum were happy to have a visitor. When Alice tried to say good-bye, they told her, "You're starting backwards! The first thing in a visit is to say hello and what your name is. That's manners!"

"I'm sorry," Alice told them. "I must be going. I'm following the White Rabbit. I'm curious to know where he's going."

"She's curious," said Tweedledum. Tweedledee nodded. "The oysters were curious, too." Tweedledum sighed.

The twins' words made Alice curious. So she stayed to listen to their story. "The Walrus and the Carpenter," began Tweedledee. "Or the story of the curious oysters," added Tweedledum.

The Walrus and the Carpenter were walking along the beach one day. The Carpenter said they could sweep all the sand off the beach, if only the Walrus would help. The Walrus didn't like to work. He quickly changed the subject to cabbages and kings and other silly things.

As they walked along, they spotted a bed of young oysters. Now, the Walrus knew a good meal when he saw it. But he had to get the oysters to leave their safe bed. The Walrus told them of the wide world they could see, if they would just follow him. The curious oysters followed him, but in a shack that the Carpenter built, the oysters became the Walrus's dinner!

"The end," said Tweedledum and Tweedledee.

"That's a very sad story," Alice said, "but I must go."

And, being as curious as the oysters, Alice left to look for the White Rabbit.

Farther into the woods, she came to a cottage. "Now, I wonder who lives here," said Alice.

To Alice's surprise, the White Rabbit ran out. "Mary Ann!" he cried. "Go get my gloves!"

Before Alice could say that she was not Mary Ann, the White Rabbit had pushed her into his house. Alice went upstairs, trying to think where a rabbit might keep gloves. She found only cookies labeled "Eat Me." Happily, Alice helped herself. Soon she felt herself growing...and growing...

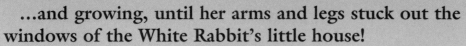

...and growing, until her arms and legs stuck out the windows of the White Rabbit's little house!

"HELP! Monster!" The White Rabbit saw the Dodo. "A monster, Dodo! In my house!"

The Dodo suggested that a chimney sweep might get Alice out of the house. Then he suggested burning the house down!

"Oh, dear, this is serious," Alice said. She plucked a carrot from the White Rabbit's garden. As soon as she ate it, she shrank.

Alice stepped outside only to see the rabbit race off again.

"I'm late, I'm late, I'm late!" he cried.

As Alice climbed down the front steps after him, the Dodo stopped her. "I say, young lady, do you have a match?"

"No, I'm sorry." Alice ran off as fast as her tiny legs would run. "I'll never catch the rabbit when I'm this small!" she gasped.

Alice stopped to catch her breath in a flower garden. She heard an insect buzz by. When she looked up, she saw that it was a rockinghorse fly!

Even more surprising, the flowers spoke to Alice! They asked what sort of bloom she was. When Alice told them that she was not a flower at all, they chased her from the garden. If she wasn't a flower, she had to be a weed!

Alice escaped from the flowers. Then, in the distance, she heard chanting. Peering through the leaves, she saw a blue caterpillar blowing smoky vowels from a water pipe. "A, E, I, O, U," he sang. "U, O, I, E, A."

When he saw Alice, he puffed out a U. "Who are you?" he asked. Alice tried to blow his smoke away from her. But her puff of breath blew the caterpillar right out of his shoes!

"Oh, dear!" said Alice as she picked up the tiny shoes. When she looked up, the caterpillar had become a butterfly!

"I have a few helpful hints," said the new butterfly. "One side will make you taller, and the other side will make you shorter."

"The other side of what?" Alice called after him.

"The mushroom, of course," the butterfly answered.

Alice pulled off two pieces of the mushroom. "I wonder which side is which," she said.

It didn't really matter, Alice decided. She had grown up and down so much lately. With a shrug, Alice bit into one of the mushroom pieces. She soon found out which piece it was.

Alice sprouted up so quickly through the trees that she caught a bird's nest in her hair!

"Serpent!" cried the mother bird.

Alice quickly bit into the other piece of mushroom. Down she shrank. "Goodness!" said Alice. "I wonder if I'll ever get the knack of it." Carefully, she gave a quick lick to the growing side of the mushroom. Finally she returned to her normal size.

Alice put the mushroom pieces in her pocket. Goodness knew when she would need them again. She began walking through the woods, looking for some sign of the White Rabbit. She did find signs, but they weren't much help. Every one pointed in a different direction. As Alice puzzled over which way to go, she heard singing.

Looking up, Alice saw a large mouth grinning down at her. Bit by bit, the body of a colorful striped cat joined his toothy smile.

"Why, you're a cat!" said Alice.

"A Cheshire cat," he answered, and disappeared again.

When he reappeared, Alice asked him for directions. The Cheshire Cat answered, "If you'd really like to know, the White Rabbit went that way."

"The White Rabbit went that way?"
Alice repeated.

"What rabbit?" asked the Cheshire Cat.
He raised his brow. "Of course, if I were
looking for a white rabbit, I'd ask the
Mad Hatter. Or there's the March Hare.
Of course, he's mad, too. Most everyone's
mad here."

Alice turned away. "Goodness," she
said, "if the people here are like that, I
must try not to upset them!"

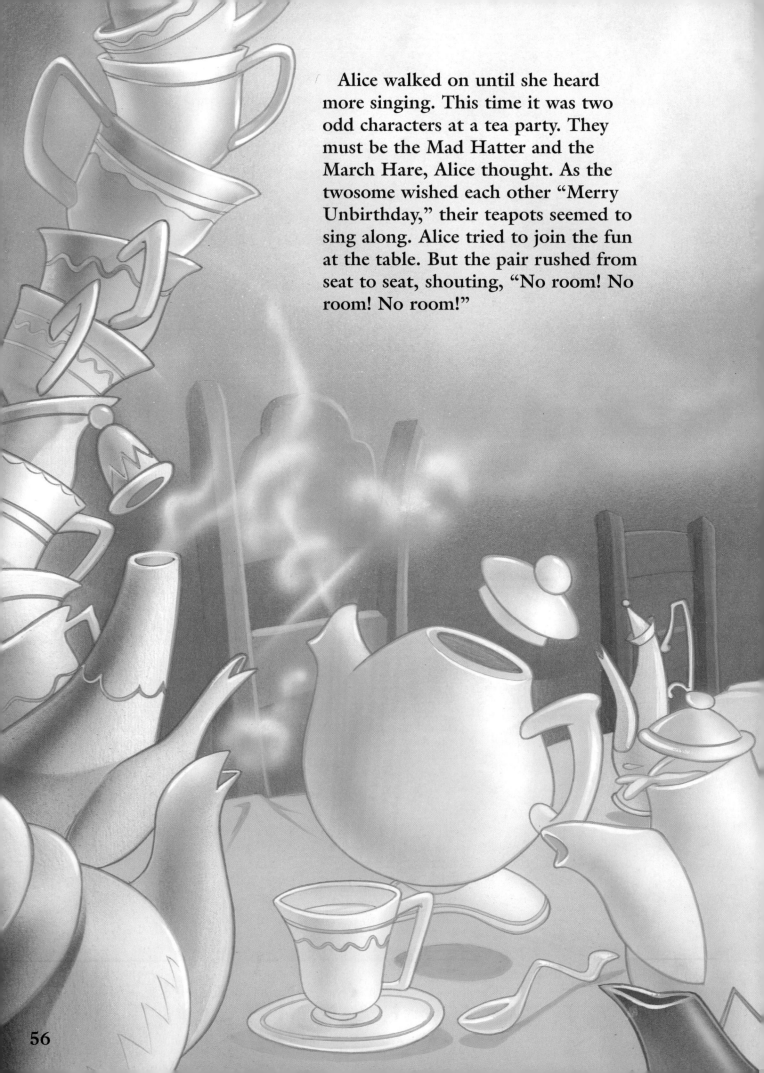

Alice walked on until she heard more singing. This time it was two odd characters at a tea party. They must be the Mad Hatter and the March Hare, Alice thought. As the twosome wished each other "Merry Unbirthday," their teapots seemed to sing along. Alice tried to join the fun at the table. But the pair rushed from seat to seat, shouting, "No room! No room! No room!"

"I'm very sorry," said Alice. "But I did enjoy your singing."

"Oh, what a delightful child!" exclaimed the Mad Hatter. "We never get compliments!"

They sat Alice at the table and offered her a cup of tea. Then they explained what an unbirthday was. "You get just one birthday every year," the March Hare began.

"But there are 364 unbirthdays!" the Mad Hatter finished.

"Why, then today is my unbirthday, too!" said Alice. "What a small world this is!" The Mad Hatter swept off his hat. There, on top of his head, was an unbirthday cake! "Now blow out the candle and make your wish," said the Mad Hatter.

When Alice blew out the candle, the cake burst into bright colors, and a dormouse parachuted down from it.

61

Suddenly the White Rabbit himself appeared.
"I'm late, I'm late, I'm late!" cried the White Rabbit.
"Well, no wonder you're late," the Mad Hatter told
him. "Your watch is exactly two days slow." The Mad
Hatter and the March Hare went to work. They
smashed the watch springs, then smeared them with
lemon and jam. Then they tossed the White Rabbit
and his watch out of their tea party!

Alice shook her head and walked away. "I've had enough nonsense," she said. "I'm going home. Who cares where the White Rabbit's going, anyway?"

But even as Alice looked for her path, a funny broom-dog brushed it away!

Strange birds surrounded Alice. She began to cry. "It would be nice if something made sense for a change!" she wailed.

Alice wished that she had never followed the White Rabbit down the rabbit hole. But more than anything else, Alice wished that she were back home. She couldn't make sense of this nonsense world at all.

Then, in a tree above, Alice heard familiar singing. It was the Cheshire Cat! Perhaps he could help. "I want to go home," Alice told him, "but I can't find my way."

"Naturally," the cat answered. "You have no way. All ways here are the Queen's ways."

"Please," said Alice, trying not to sniffle, "how can I find her?"

The cat opened a door and Alice stepped through.

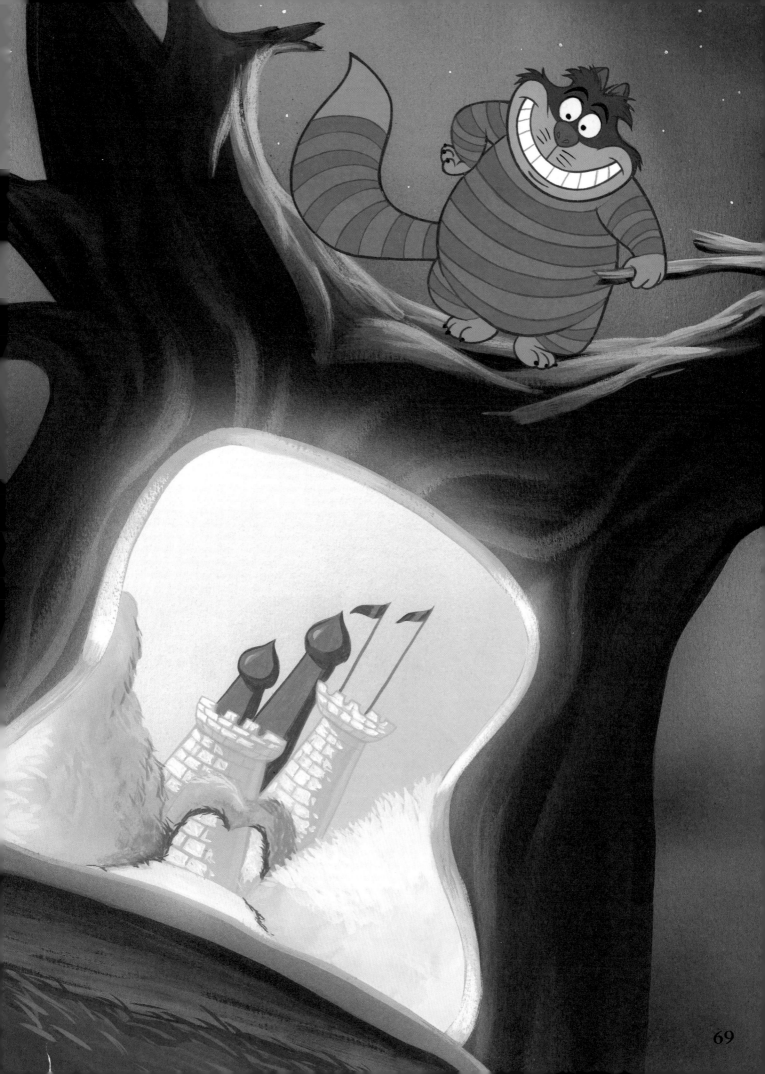

Alice soon learned that everyone was afraid of the Queen and her terrible temper. In the royal garden, card soldiers secretly painted the roses red. They had planted white roses by mistake, and if the Queen saw even one white rose, they could lose their heads! Alice was helping them paint when a trumpet sounded.

The White Rabbit raced into view. The
playing cards formed a royal arch. Perhaps,
Alice thought as she watched, this is why the
White Rabbit kept saying he was late. He wouldn't
want to be late to announce the Queen.
No one would want to be late to announce the Queen.

"Her Royal Majesty! The Queen of Hearts!" called the rabbit.
The cards cheered as the Queen entered. Trailing behind her,
the King cleared his throat.

"And the King," the White Rabbit added.

Alice's was the only voice that cheered for the King.

The Queen soon spotted Alice. "Why, it's a little girl! Now where are you from and where are you going?" Before Alice could answer, the Queen added, "Speak nicely, turn out your toes, curtsy, and always say, 'Yes, Your Majesty.'"

Alice did as she was told, and said, "I'm trying to find my way home."

"*Your* way!" the Queen shouted. "All ways here are *my* ways!"

Alice tried to explain, but the Queen changed the subject. "Do you play croquet?" she asked.

The Queen was very pleased when Alice curtsied and said, "Yes, Your Majesty."

The Queen loved to play croquet. No matter how badly she swung her flamingo mallet or how badly she hit the hedgehog ball, the cards always made sure she won. For if the Queen lost her game, they lost their heads!

As the Queen prepared to swing, the Cheshire Cat appeared.

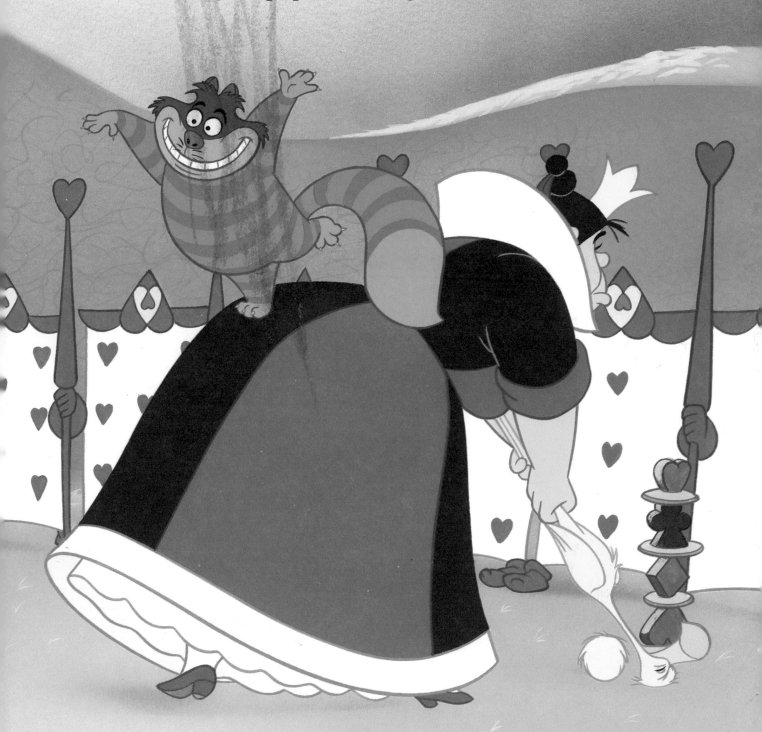

Only Alice saw the Cheshire Cat. "You know," he said to Alice, "we could make her really angry."

"Oh, no!" said Alice. "Stop!"

The Cheshire Cat just grinned. He tangled the Queen's mallet in her skirt. When the Queen went to swing, she flopped down, and her skirt flapped up.

"Oh, my fur and whiskers!" said the White Rabbit.

The Queen heaved herself up with the help of the cards. "Someone's head will roll for this!" she bellowed. She pointed at Alice. "Yours!"

Of course, the Cheshire Cat had disappeared.

The King piped up. "Couldn't she have a trial first?"

The Queen humphed, but said yes. The King and the cards cheered as the trial began.

The White Rabbit read the charge against Alice: She had caused the Queen of Hearts to lose her temper.

"Ready for your sentence?" the Queen asked Alice.

"Sentence?" said Alice. "But there must be a verdict first."

"Sentence first!" the Queen thundered. But then she agreed to let the March Hare and the Mad Hatter appear as witnesses. They didn't help Alice at all. But they did start an unbirthday tea party for the King and the Queen.

The Queen enjoyed her unbirthday party. Then she announced Alice's sentence. "Off with her head!"

Alice reached into her pockets and put both mushroom pieces in her mouth. She grew until she towered over the Queen.

"I'm not afraid of you!" she said. "You're a pompous, bad-tempered tyrant!"

But even as she spoke, Alice shrank until she was smaller than the Queen.

"Off with her head!" the Queen shouted once
more. The cards closed in around Alice. The full
deck followed her as she raced away into a maze. In,
out, left, right, Alice twisted her way through the
maze. With one quick turn, she found herself
running over the cards. Alice slipped off their shiny
backs and out of the maze. Then she was back in the
Dodo's race!

As Alice ran down the beach, she met the Mad Hatter and the March Hare. "Join us in a cup of tea," said the March Hare.

All three of them fell into a giant cup. Alice pulled herself free and saw the Caterpillar floating in the water.

"Mister Caterpillar, what will I do?" wailed Alice. The Caterpillar blew a smoke ring at her. In the wisps of smoke, Alice saw the Doorknob. As she ran toward it, she grew larger with each step.

"Still locked, you know," the Doorknob told her.

As Alice tugged on the Doorknob, the
Queen, the cards, the March Hare, and the
Mad Hatter were right behind her! She
could hear the Queen shouting for her head.

"The Queen!" Alice gasped. "I simply
must get out!"

"But you are outside," the Doorknob
told her.

Alice peered through the keyhole. She did
see herself outside! She was asleep, with
Dinah on her lap.

"Alice, wake up!" Alice shouted to herself.

"Alice!" Alice's sister woke her. "Pay attention to your lesson."

Alice jumped up and looked around. No Queen was shouting for her head. No cards were chasing her. The birds had only feathers. The flowers did not talk. The nonsense world was gone!

"Come along." Her sister closed the book. "It's time for tea."

Alice followed her sister happily. She was home, and a no-nonsense cup of tea awaited her.

Thank goodness!